RE: MARRIAGE

For Jeff —
Read it + weep.
John ...

5/9/07

also by John Norton:

Posthum(or)ous
The Light at the End of the Bog
(American Book Award)

RE: MARRIAGE

John Norton

Black Star Series ▸ San Francisco

Copyright 2000   ISBN 0-9607630-5-8

Designed by Anne Subercaseaux

Distributed by
Small Press Distribution
1341 Seventh Street
Berkeley, CA 94114

www.spdbooks.org

PREFACE

whomever I love
in most instances
I continue to love
you the exception
tuning you out now
new love comes into frame
everything ties together
associations persist
the real drops away

In LA everyone has a story to sell and a screenplay to pitch. Mine is how an academic marriage finishes in near-violence. The story unfolds within a series of flashbacks. I get more than halfway through a draft when the characters turn hyperreal. Old conversations replay incessantly, and it finally sinks in that there will be no reconciliation. There is no new love at hand to replace the old, either. This cool LA life is quickly eroding and once again I feel overwhelmed. I consider then reject moving back to Boston. What's the point to living in LA unless you're in the movie business.

Divorce was the breakpoint. The decree became final in the Madison Family Court after I moved to California. That was 1966. I was almost thirty. Two years later I was living in Beverly Hills and began a screen treatment about Paul, his wife Pauline, Laura, and those smug inhabitants of the Philosophy Department. Coincidentally, "Who's Afraid of Virginia Woolf" was playing at the Bruin, a first-run cinema in Westwood. My comment on the film: "Too much like life." The woman I saw the film with (I can't recall her name) asked why.

I never went back to that script. The project, like many others, remains unfinished. Relationships form and fade over twenty years. A career change. A move to the Bay Area. California is now home but nothing here remains static state.

San Francisco
Monday, September 19, 1988　　　　　　　　*11:30 AM*

The morning reading on public radio is a selection from Edith Wharton's letters. I listen to her fuss in her passionate love for Morton Fullerton. Fretting when they are apart. Pleading for more time together. Passion inevitably declines and her recriminations begin. 'You never loved me . . . you ignored my desire to be with you.' I've been accused of that. She could be generous. She interrupted work on a novel to advise others how to write. She could be curt. She scolds a young writer for wasting her time. 'Stop sending me manuscripts,' she writes, 'stop wasting your time. Writing your life does not make it a novel, nor constitute a novel.' She'd have snatched the pen from his hand. The reading closes with a note from Wharton's secretary writing some years after the affair ended, asking Fullerton to return the letters, as if retracting them would efface the record of their relationship. She's unpredictable.

Cold coming on. Shut the door! Tense. Shoulders stiff. The dead feeling. I miss long walks by the Bay. I used to live with Susan in an airy Art Deco condo near the Bay. Mind emptying walks. Water and seabirds, the brown Marin hills patched with clusters of live oaks on the other side of the Bay, a rust-orange bridge spanning the Gate. Some years ago to lift myself out of the morass I was in I began walking. A brother had recently died. My sister Peggy lay ill in Boston with breast cancer. Unemployed.

In less than two years I lost three jobs. Three or four mornings a week I'd set out, briskly walking the shoreline then without slowing stride up and down the Presidio's hills. The demons would materialize. I'd curse them, sometimes startling the joggers by cursing aloud. Former bosses. An ex-wife and her lover. People who did me wrong. The enemies list. Walking them out of my system. Walking out of that relationship with Susan.

The outer circumstances of life have changed yet too much feels the same. Slam that door shut! I live alone. Not enough physical contact with women. Present life is empty of lovers and my imagination turns to past relationships - how we thrived at first, how we drew apart. Laura. Susan. The end of a relationship seems to characterize it. Elaine may join the list. Just phoned home to check the answering machine. There are no messages.

If I focus on what happened, if I say that on the third Monday in January at three in the afternoon this took place, or on Monday, March first, about ten in the morning there was another crisis, if I keep summing up what has gone on, then I prove to myself and anyone else who cares to listen that I am *not* going mad. Ranting the chronology, taking notes when I recall more, fitting everything into the right sequence all help. I tell everyone what is happening: my family, Laura's mother, her sister Hanna, a priest in Madison, another in Boston who was evaluating Laura's petition for an annulment, a shrink in California, my friend Bob, Laura's friends, former neighbors of the Masons whom I meet by chance one afternoon in Rittenhouse Square when I had returned to Philadelphia for my oral exams. We can make unreasonable demands on confidants: demand they take our side completely, share our bruised feelings, adopt our anger toward the person or persons who injure us — just as if they also have been injured. I became an evangelist of pain.

So Laura has moved on! So she's living with Paul and his children! I still want her. You can lust for a woman and still hate her guts. *Want to fuck her good and fuck her hard.*

After Laura moved out I had time to think how I might kill Paul. Run him down and squash him under the wheels of a blue VW bug. Push him down a flight of stairs, stomp on his face, lay into him like Jack Palance. I make a sick joke.

"What do you call a philosopher who lies?"

"I don't know."

What do you call a philosopher who lies?"

"A *good* philosopher."

I am left with an awful mixture of self-loathing and envy. Before most of this began, I signed a contract to teach in California. It is now time to leave. I fly into LAX in late September one week before classes start. My anger hot and close as the suffocating smog.

The past sometimes resurfaces, quite differently from when those events were unfolding, when without prodding I'd tell the world what was happening, citing the day of the week and time of day when each cruel incident occurred. Once knowing well the sequence of those events kept me close to reality. My life was chaos. Order, if any, lay in the details.

San Francisco
Wednesday, September 21 *6:00 PM*

Second day off from work with this cold. Feeling more energy, I called Elaine early this morning. We meet at a Noe Valley deli. Elaine arrives from her exercise class. She smells clean. We sit outdoors at a table in the courtyard. Slowly getting to know her again — there was a six-month gap. After three canceled dates I broke contact. Once she changed her mind about going out as I arrive at her front door. Said she wanted to stay home alone. I turned and left, then became infuriated on the way back home. I wrote Elaine an angry letter but never mailed it. The woman still attracts me though I fret over my unreturned calls. Lunch and we talk about many

*things. For example, love and dominance. Elaine is
reading a critical biography of Picasso. She says Picasso
abused his wives. I say I know someone like that.
I outline a few episodes of how Paul applied his academic
leverage to conquer a series of female students, including
Laura, when I was married to her. Desire is intrinsic to the
learning process. Elaine listens.*

The helicopter moves like an awkward beast, a giant grasshopper with rotor props fore and aft. The blades chug and then start spinning, whipping up dust and papers from the LAX tarmac. We taxi away from the terminal. Vibrations register in every tooth. The unsteady motion and whirring reminding me of a scene witnessed in a Boston laundromat. Two rows of pink and yellow Speed Queens bouncing in erratic rhythms after some street punks lifted the machines off their mounts. We are twelve hundred feet above the San Bernardino freeway and heading east. The purple San Gabriel mountains off to the left behind a dirty butterscotch haze. Below us the incessant traffic. One city blending into another. In the late summer evening, grids of street lights, nine blocks at a time, popping on at random. We descend next to a shopping mall in Pomona and drop off two passengers. The rotors keep moving in a slower spin. The cabin door folds back in, the vibrations resume, and we're abruptly up and off. Amber pin lights punctuate the herring-bone striped parking lots. "Next stop Ontario," says the pilot over the PA. Freed from storage in memory the sardonic voice of the Union Station trainmaster on the Jack Benny radio show announces with prolonged rolling vowels the departure call for *Pasadena Azusa Pomona Ontario and Cucamonga*. That last stop always exaggerated. *Cu-ca-mon-ga. Monga, mambo, tango.* I concatenated the sounds. I saw the crowd dancing as the train pulled into the depot. This helicopter is taking me fifteen miles further east to the near edge of the Southern California desert. "Next stop Riverside," says the pilot over the PA. I alight. The helicopter lifts off again in a whirl of hot dust, pushing the tumbleweeds against the chain-link fence then heads east towards Palm Springs. The sign at the heliport:

WELCOME TO RIVERSIDE
HOME OF THE ORIGINAL
NAVEL ORANGE TREE

Wednesday, cont'd.

She continues to inhabit my subconscious. I sometimes dream of her yet never visualize her features. Her face remains hidden in shadows or she is turning away. She never looks directly at me. Dreams are our best guide to the past. When I moved to California, I left the wedding pictures and our college yearbook behind. Stuffed them into a kitchen cabinet for the next tenant to wonder about. Laura's image has faded though strongly felt memories of our marriage and divorce remain. They surface unexpectedly, like today at lunch.

Imagine the next couple finding the album upon moving in. They bring it out one night during a party. Everyone's heard about the abandoned wedding album. They ask the guests to act out the marriage of David and Laura. Imagine that.

Thursday, September 22   3:00 PM

Elaine gave wonderful advice at Tuesday's lunch. We were talking about love and dominance. She kept paraphrasing from a recent biography that described how Picasso treated his wives. He looked to dominate their psyches and undo them. I mentioned I knew such a person once — the philosopher Paul Mason who drew Laura away from me. "He was very conscious of his power over women," I told Elaine. I acknowledged that Laura and Paul married. "Why don't you write about them," Elaine said. "Maybe," I said, "maybe my feelings about the events are unresolved. It's difficult to shape those memories into a story. I tried, you know. There's an unfinished screenplay in the file cabinet." Because the events and people still stir me I should write about them. This is Elaine's advice. "Go for the charge," she urges me.

After lunch I walked back over the hill to the Cafe Flore, found an outdoor table free, and began writing. "Laura and I married in Boston in the early sixties. We were two years out of college."

Friday, September 23   *1:30 PM*

Today's mail brings a postcard from Elaine. A photo portrait of Yeats. She copied the following lines on the back.

> Does the imagination dwell the most
> Upon a woman won or a woman lost?
>
> "The Tower"

For a long period after the divorce, many women reminded me of Laura. It could be the texture of hair as I ran my fingers through it or a secondary reaction after making casual eye contact on the street. The smell of Chanel trailing after her. The curve of a back. The low-pitched laugh overheard in a darkened theater. Laura is immanent. Occasionally I would see her.

The journey west. Between the time I interview for the job and when I show up in California, my life turns over. I arrive in California knowing no one, just those two senior faculty who interviewed me months earlier at the Modern Language Association meetings in New

York. Neither is particularly friendly. I dub one the Green Man to honor his liking for polyester. He assesses your worth by the length of your bibliography. Nothing personal. Do everything in a couple of days. Find an apartment. Buy a car. Make new friends. Get laid. Prepare my classes and start teaching.

I drop in on Riverside like a paratrooper. The vegetation feels alien. Iceplant. Dichondra. Yucca. Unfamiliar names. The campus an intellectual ghost town. The torrid sun drives everyone indoors. Seldom another pedestrian. The city appears depopulated. Brownish air spiked with ozone. Everyone in chopped cars cruising behind darkened windows. Custom mufflers purring. I spend my first week at the Mission Inn, an accretion of Spanish Revival in downtown Riverside. The Inn was built to help make Riverside famous and both had seen better times. Nixon and Pat married in the chapel and honeymooned at the Inn, according to a plaque on the lobby wall. It amuses me to think that creature was loved. Another self-absorbed prick.

Memories darken the strong Southern California sun. I'm abruptly back in Madison mumbling. There's more to say. I meet Bert, a sweet man from a nearby college. His strong features remind me of Paul's. I go to Bert's poetry reading, not really hearing him, but imagine getting up on the platform to interrupt his talk and smash that face. Whose face? I can't say.

Alternating stubby and gangly palm trees along Riverside city streets. Ridiculous vegetation with one exception. The sharp medicinal smell of the eucalyptus in the hot sunshine. Unfamiliar landmarks. New England has a more reasonable scale: elms, maples, rolled green lawns bordered with manicured hedges. That familiar green of nature not present here on the edge of the desert.

New England

set in granite
locked by place
taut and certain

redfaced lobsterman
bent over the gunwale
hauling traps

as they are
not becoming
not about to change

the spit of land
called Bearskin Neck

having obligations
to worship and heed

the staid exterior
the family set
for life

iron-smooth tide
cries of gulls
wheeling

This landscape makes one feel insigificant.

No one grasps what I have just been through. I make an appointment with a friendly MD. On the phone, I tell him I have a cough that won't stop. In the examination room, I reveal why I am there. I am looking for a therapist.

"I've just been through a divorce, Doc." I start my screed. "She never trusted anyone. She kept accusing me of sleeping with other women. I could have used the sex and she was sleeping with another man."

He pays attention.

"Anyone call tell what happened just by looking at me, as if there's a D stamped on my forehead."

His face remains expressionless.

"I failed and everyone can see that. I'm as obvious as Hester Prynne with her embroidered A."

"Do I know her, David?"

I shake my head to say *No* and keep any doubts about California to myself.

"It was like 'Virginia Woolf.'"

"Who's that?"

"That's a play in New York about a ferocious academic couple called George and Martha. Soon to be a movie with Elizabeth Taylor and Richard Burton. Natural casting."

He's evaluating me.

"I don't have much time for the movies, David. What happened to you back there in Madison doesn't show. If you want someone to talk to, I'll give you names to call."

It's twenty-five years after Laura and I graduated and I am back in Boston for a funeral. I take a break from closing my sister Peggy's apartment and drive down to Cape Cod to visit some college friends. Jim and Margaret Anne married right after graduation and remain together. We have not seen each other in many years; they very warmly welcome me. The Murphys have six children, their oldest daughter's already completed college. Jim's a writer. Margaret Anne went back to school and became a family therapist. Jim and I exchange books. A collection of my poems for a copy of his novel. She builds a fire and serves coffee with brandy. We talk about books and teaching, writers we dislike, and what makes a good marriage. Jim walks over to the bookcase and brings back our class yearbook. Right away I look up Laura. She is in a half dozen pictures. There is her Bachrach portrait, which I keep going back to. Here's Laura with the Dramatic Society playing Katherina in "The Taming of the Shrew" and a few pages later another picture. Treasurer of the Philosophy Club. "Christ, Jim! I haven't seen this face in years. She's lovely." When we met, I felt Laura was my best chance for love. Laura and I are in the group photo of the *Stylus*, an undergraduate magazine. I forgot about that. There are no other photos of us together. It is after eleven when I leave.

On the drive back to Boston, a sense of great loss sweeps over me. The women in my life desert me. I push a tape of the Brahms piano concerto into the deck. Take a couple of tokes on a joint. Those pictures. She was beautiful.

Friends give occasional reports. Like drums in jungle movies, the academic grapevine never stops. I might have told them *Stop. It's over. Don't bother me with that* but didn't.

Laura and I married in the early sixties, two years out of college. We have a vision (let's call it fantasy) of transcending the sentimentalizing that hobbles our families. Our ideal merges intellectual with romantic life. We marry in late June and within two months leave for Philadelphia to start graduate school. Laura's choice is Philosophy. I study literature. A cynical friend (now a former friend) called us bookish misfits, looking to fulfill each others' yearnings for sex and romance.

In her second year at Penn Laura joined Paul's circle of students. Paul is charismatic. He challenges heads-on the Department's uptight faculty and disparages their sense of propriety as well as their intelligence. He makes a point of never wearing a tie and dressing the same everyday, whether meeting the dean or his classes, in a blue velour shirt with a Navy blazer, pressed chinos and loafers. He has multiple copies of each item and would show off his wardrobe to visitors. Paul's features are bony. Olive skin stretched tight over his skull. I have no problem recalling *his* features. Graying hair cut short. Black bushy brows over deep-set always moving brown eyes. Frank Ramsey used to cite Russell's quip that Paul has the eyes of a con man.

Paul is the subject of rumors. He attracts a series of young women. Some flee. Marilyn transferred to Cornell. Gladys left for the Peace Corps. Joan was seeing Paul and another man, then married a foreign student and decided to move to Italy with him.

There are occasional parties at the Masons' home where faculty and grad students get together to drink and talk shop. I observe how Paul makes sure the focus stays on him. His thick voice amplifies the natural inflections found in a sentence. Intonation never too strong or weak. Even when he masks his words in irony, even then he wants them considered seriously, perhaps literally, if you are gullible enough.

The Francis Bacon dual portrait of the Masons is the centerpiece in their living room. A tawny-colored block with thick lines represents Paul's head. A string of gray spirals for hair. Ombre patches for eyes. Pauline's figure is less defined. Her gaze focuses on a point somewhere beyond the viewer's left shoulder. She's not "there."

"I write to music and can recall which pieces were playing on the stereo as I wrote the individual chapters." Paul is standing in front of the fireplace, one foot on the hearthstone. The portrait is behind him. Everyone faces Paul.

Pauline grimaces. She is in the audience, standing next to Laura. "God, I hated the Sibelius chapter, day after day after day after day." She fakes a sad face. "Serious." She puts fingers into the two corners of her mouth and pulls her lips and cheeks down into a clownishly gloomy face. "*Very* serious."

When they perform, Pauline sings harmony.

"Bach carried me as I was writing about synonymy." Pauline hums a phrase from *Finlandia*. She's still working the previous metaphor. Paul resumes, "Each sentence parallels a musical phrase. I formulated the thesis to the Brandenburg Concertos and wrote the rebuttals of Quine and Goodman in descending eighths. Rephrased their counter arguments as minor chords. Statement, clarification, resolution — all coming together in the finale."

"Finally," Pauline says, "a change of music."

Paul is toying with us. If he can subjugate Bach, one of the Masters, he is capable of devastating lesser challengers. That's what he wants us to realize. Paul catches me looking at him.

"Another drink, David?"

"I've had enough."

He won't break eye contact.

"Pauline, get David another drink."

Pauline heads for the kitchen — humming.

"Anything else, David?"

There is a trace of a smile. Paul turns back to his group.

We are influenced by others' marriages. We witness our parents'. Friends confide in us. Laura and I take the Pennsy Main Line local out to Bryn Mawr to see the Masons. Paul and Pauline visit our apartment near Rittenhouse Square. After dinner, we'd go to the movies. Ours is a couples friendship. The Masons are a central couple. Freud observed how many share the marriage bed.

Laura's parents visit us in Philadelphia. Marlene is clearly disappointed with the second-hand furniture. She worries aloud about the black neighbors. She wants to know "why there are no pictures of God in the house." The next day Marlene buys a gilt-framed lithograph of the Virgin treading on a male serpent. She is ready to hang it herself until I stop her.

"I'll do that later. I promise," as I prop the holy picture against the baseboard.

Tom is watching TV. "She brought it to a rectory to have it blessed."

"Thanks a lot."

"You'll probably hear from the priests."

"Thanks again."

After they leave I stuff it into a closet. They won't visit here again.

Fragments of a story, an unfinished script, scenes waiting for a final runthrough. The locale is a large white framed house surrounded by a well trimmed lawn with an English-style rose garden. The Masons are hosting a summer wedding. Zeno, a former Jesuit, is about to marry Giuliana, an exotic woman from Sao Paulo. His second marriage and her first. Giuliana is sensual. Her round hips and large soft breasts undulate in a pale blue silk sheath. There are wet patches under her arms. Her flowing gestures contradict Zeno's controlled, ascetic mannerisms. Zeno may be phobic. In fifty years, he likes to argue, people will take to small private rooms to eat, as if they are going to the bathroom. He defends the proposition with great vigor.

A heavyset judge from the Pennsylvania Common Pleas Court gives me the hand signal to start walking towards him. I'm to give the bride away. Paul and Laura are the witnesses. Paul stands next to Zeno, who is chatting with Joan in the front row. Giuliana and I walk arm in arm under the flowering wisteria. Zeno and Paul meet us in front of the judge. Paul removes my arm from Giuliana's and replaces it with Zeno's. Up to the start of the ceremony and beyond, Pauline stays busy with the details of the reception: supervising the two student bartenders, who are lining up the glasses and sampling the champagne, directing the hired caterer and waitresses, shooing away Sammy the Siamese cat.

The judge motions for us to gather in a semicircle. Marilyn, Joan and Claudio, me, a few faculty, Michael and Caroline Mason, Paul's students, and some neighbors. His Honor's words resound. Even with this heat and humidity and since he was paid for it, he does the full ceremony, closing with "By the authority vested in me by the Commonwealth of Pennsylvania and the laws of God (the quaint phrasing generates a round of eye contact among the philosophers) I declare you man and wife, until death do you part." Their professional skepticism now a mannerism.

While all are congratulating Zeno and Giuliana and the waitresses are distributing champagne for the toast, Sammy trots out from under the hedge carrying a trophy in her mouth. She lays it at the judge's feet. The judge shakes Zeno's hand and gives the bride a peck on her right cheek. A monogrammed handkerchief appears from under his robes to mop the sweat from his forehead. Pauline shrieks, "David, please get rid of that." I use a cocktail napkin to pick the shredded mole up by its tail and whirl it over the fence into a neighboring yard.

In October Paul accepts a job offer from Madison. Academics routinely move on. No unanticipated move, though, passes by without generating comment. The graduate students begin gossiping about why Paul is leaving Penn. He is not getting promoted to full professor. He got a student pregnant. He had a *you go* or *I go* argument with Goodman over who would teach aesthetics.

Pauline stays away from the campus. She knows about younger women's attraction to Paul. In June, after school was out, Pauline flies to Madison to organize the move. Within two weeks she finds a house with a lease purchase option in University Heights, a section of Madison where tenured faculty lived, and enrolls Michael and Caroline in the junior high. She returns to Philadelphia, more than enthusiastic over the cathedral ceilings and air conditioning waiting for the family in Madison.

Another year at Penn for Laura and me. Laura is writing the second draft of the dissertation. I'm studying for doctoral exams. The Masons are still in my life. In Madison, Paul has persuaded the Department to hire Laura. Over the next Labor Day weekend Laura and I drive the thousand miles from Philadelphia to Madison with Henry the cat howling from under the front seat. Laura's classes will start in less than two weeks. Pauline found an apartment for us on Madison's east side. We buy a day bed, borrow a card table and folding chairs. It is like setting up a field camp. Pauline says she will do everything to help Laura feel comfortable in Madison. "You'll be part of the family while David is away," she says. I'm flying back to Philadelphia, where I am completing the research for my dissertation and jobhunting. Before I leave in the morning, Laura measures the windows for curtains.

The next three months I commute between Madison and Philadelphia. I go to Iowa City and Milwaukee to interview for jobs I really didn't want, then fly on to Madison to spend long weekends with Laura before returning to Philadelphia. We makes plans to meet in Boston for Thanksgiving with her parents.

Laura's parents talk without metaphor. They exchange information not feelings.

"I'm fixing chicken for supper."

"I work swing Friday to cover for Ray."

"There's a good show on seven."

"Let's go see the Christmas lights in Winchester."

Marlene's need for control is relentless. Tom's a little dopey from nipping on cough medicine laced with codeine. Marlene never forgives him for past binges and constantly reminds him how much he owes her. She kept the home together while he drank. She made sure the mortgage got paid. She wrote the checks for Laura's tuition. I tune her out. Tom keeps nursing that cough.

I let everyone know there is a chance of a job in California. Our stay in Madison may be brief. While Laura and I are unpacking the boxes shipped from Philadelphia, I spot Paul's name on some notes left on her desk. I look again but they are gone. Laura doesn't want to celebrate the holidays alone so she organizes a New Year's Eve party. Paul and Pauline arrive early. I invite someone from the English Department and his wife. The group gathers around Paul as he relays his best gossip from the Winter Philosophy Meetings. The focus is still on him. When the ice runs out, Paul volunteers, "I'll drive home for more." Laura bundles up in her mouton coat. "I'll go with Paul." With my eyes I ask Pauline what is happening. She reveals nothing.

Paul encourages me to apply to the Wisconsin English Department. I mail a letter and resumé to the Chairman. Paul says he'll pass on any news through Laura. In about two weeks, a response from the English Department arrives. They decided not to interview me and wish me well in the job search. I feel relieved. I am uncomfortable in Madison. Something is changing or has already changed. The cat gets kidney stones. Another whopping vet bill.

Laura and I are at home. She's unusually tense. It's as if I am impinging on her. Three weeks into the new year and on a Monday afternoon there is an emergency call from Boston. Laura's father collapsed after shoveling out the driveway. She is Tom's favorite. I drive to the university to find Laura and meet Paul on the way to her class. He wants to know why I am looking for her, so I tell him. We wait outside the lecture room for her class to end, and I repeat what her mother said. Paul hovers outside Laura's office while she calls the hospital in Cambridge. Laura begins to cry. Tom is dead from cardiac arrest. We'll be in Boston the following day.

Tuesday morning. Pauline drives us to the airport. She and Laura are wearing the same type of black mouton coat. They chat about the children. Pauline will have Michael come by to feed the cat. From my perspective in the back seat they look related.

Tom worked for the telephone company. He looked forward to an early retirement after three more years on the assembly line. Tom worked for the color TV, the electric lawn mower, the new house and car. Marlene regulates the rest of their life. Cards and coffee with the Lombardis on Saturday nights. Nine o'clock Mass every Sunday. Dinner once a month at the Hilltop in Saugus, where the prime rib arrives draped over the sides of the plate and the oversized baked potatoes look like aluminized ostrich eggs. Tom's last binge started at Hanna's wedding. After that episode Marlene kept tighter rein on him. She made sure, for instance, that no alcohol would be served at our wedding. No big deal. There were drunks in my family, too.

Just two months earlier, Laura flew in from Madison and I drove up to Boston to spend Thanksgiving with Tom and Marlene. We are chatting over second helpings of lemon meringue pie in Marlene's kitchen, when she says that she made only one mistake in her life.

"What was that, Marlene?" I ask, sort of anticipating the answer.

She points down the hallway to the den where Tom is watching the Bruins play the Maple Leafs on TV.

"Marrying him." Now he is dead.

I try to get Laura to make love. Her body has curled into a tight ball and there's a muffled "No, I can't tonight." I go to the bathroom to jack off. In the morning Marlene focuses on getting her hair done for the wake. There's a special trip to Pilgrim Mall in Waltham for black dresses.

Marlene and Tom's style of relating affects my marriage; it develops into what philosophers call a "negative instance." Laura never trusts me. She goes through the list of women I know at Penn. "Are you sleeping with Pat?" "How attractive is Betsy? Do you want to sleep with her, too?" In the six years I live with Laura, she periodically repeats what Marlene told her. "'Never trust anyone. Then they can't hurt you.'"

We return to Madison the morning after Tom's funeral. That job in California comes through. We will leave Wisconsin. Laura starts her search for a position in Southern California (that was our agreement). Her academic references are outstanding and she has two published articles. Within weeks she has a year's contract from UCLA. She resigns from Madison, effective in June. At UCLA Laura will teach a graduate seminar in her specialty (the ethics of language) and two survey courses.

The frigid winter persists. Colder than any I experienced in Boston. A series of snowstorms and near-Arctic weather keep us indoors. Laura remains tense. I am bored. But we are about to exchange sub-zero Wisconsin for Southern California sunshine. The prospect of change helps. I'll be out of here by the end of June

Friday, cont'd.

Elaine has provoked me into writing. For three days I've relived how my marriage became enmeshed with the Masons's. This time more of what happened gets on

paper. I revisit when Laura and I met, how Paul gained Laura's affection, and the despair that followed Pauline's death. When I came home from the Cafe Flore near Thursday midnight, the message light on the answering machine was blinking. I hit the playback button. "This doesn't sound like the person I'm looking for. I'm calling David James Ryan. This is Laura. I think you know who I am. I'm in New York. My phone number is 516-555-3837. If this is not whom I'm looking for, sorry about that." The first time I hear that voice in twenty-two years. The tone sounds arch. Her diction formal academic. Remote. East Coast.

I replay the tape a couple of times. I want her voice to sink in. If Laura hadn't identified herself, perhaps I might not have recognized her. Perhaps. In those first few months after the divorce, my sense of location had yet to move with the rest of me to California. I used to fantasize about getting a call from Laura. She would call to admit she made a mistake. She'd call to ask me to take her back. The call never came, so I'd dial Paul's house in Madison, hoping Laura would answer. "Hello. . . . Hello. Who's there?" I'd put my hand over the mouthpiece and wait for her to hang up. Eventually I stop calling. Her voice fades. It is now 3:00 AM her time. The bitch can lose sleep. I call her back.

I relay my enthusiasm over hearing from her, especially, I tell her, since I've been writing a story about us. She doesn't seem surprised that I've called back. I tell Laura how a conversation with a friend provoked me into writing and say her spirit, Paul's, and Pauline's have been visiting me. D: "It's uncanny. I'm writing a story about Madison. I visualize you as I write — sometimes my memory is blocked — and suddenly you are back in my life again. But, Laura, why after all this time — it's at least twenty-two years — why call now? I don't get it." L: "I'm contacting the people who did me in." D: "What? Who did you in, Laura?" L: "You, David, you did me in." This is her agenda in calling. Laura starts to berate me. She has compiled a list of my crimes: not moving with her to Madison, not going to church with her in Philadelphia, etc. "I was a virgin when I married you. You pinched me, David, and I've never been able to let a man touch me since." Must have been a hell of a pinch. Just two years ago at Christmas my friend Bob wrote that Laura remarried again and was doing well.

Monday, March 1, just after ten in the morning. It's fifteen degrees and windy. Laura unexpectedly appears across the street from Rasmussen's Pharmacy. I finish my coffee and Danish, gear up for the cold and head outside. Laura has already met her eight o'clock class. She rushes across State Street, paying no attention to the traffic or cold. Her coat is unbuttoned and she speaks hurriedly.

"Did you hear what happened to Pauline?"

"She killed herself." Pauline's death comes as no surprise.

"How did you find out?" Laura is staring at me. "Who told you? Who else knows?"

I want to say "Just intuition" but don't. Laura is too critical to accept that. But it is intuition.

When I was a child, I used to watch my mother read fortunes in tea leaves. She did it for entertainment. She would sit at the kitchen table, empty the teacup, turn it over, spin it three times counterclockwise, wait for the liquid to drain then turn the cup back up. She discerned figures and signs in the leaves. My sisters crowded next to her. As she identified something, I'd ask where it was.

"I don't see it, Ma."

"It's right here, Davey," and with the tip of the teaspoon she'd point to the speck of leaves in question. I am barely a head taller than the table. She'd tip the cup. "Can't you see it now."

One night she saw the figure of a man's head slumped into its torso. This forecast a death according to my mother. It happened within the month when Charlie McGowan, a neighbor's son, suddenly died. The prescience frightens my mother. She never read fortunes again, as far as I recall.

Only Laura's questions surprise me.

"Who told you about Pauline?'

"The signs were there to be read," I tell her.

―――――――――――――――――――――

Friday, cont'd.

Laura starts to rake me over for badmouthing her. She says I let everyone know of her affair with Paul and destroyed her reputation. Without hesitating I tell her Fuck off! *and hang up. I pace about this small house, talking to myself. I worked to get her out of my life, put myself through years of mournful self-pity — unnecessarily. She's going on about stuff that happened almost twenty-five years ago. Does she really think I'll believe she's lived since then without intimacy or sex? That's bullshit. Neither can I wait to tell someone about this call. I'll phone Elaine in the morning, tell her about the story in progress and the phone call. "Synchronicity at work," I'll say, "her timing is uncanny."*

―――――――――――――――――――――

Only after the fact did most find out how thoroughly Pauline plotted the scenario of her suicide. She researched the Madison hardware stores for the right weight of rope, one that could support her. She wanted to be sure the cord wouldn't snap. Over lunch with her neighbors

Amos and Sarah, Pauline demonstrated how strong the rope would have to be. Amos showed the coroner's jury how Pauline would take samples from her shoulder bag and test them by tying a slip knot, placing one foot inside the loop, and pulling up sharply. The weaker ropes snapped. He remembers her saying, "If you tell anyone, I'll buy a gun and do it this afternoon." Amos was in Geology. He recalls Pauline asking him where to find rock-climbing rope. There are cliffs in Wisconsin.

There are three lunches. She tells them about Paul and Laura. One time Sarah served fettucini with string squash, hoping to distract Pauline from her melodrama. They try to get her into therapy, but no. Pauline recruits Amos and Sarah. Sucks them in.

Michael found his mother. He was getting ready for school. The door to the cellar was open and the light on. Michael went down the stairs calling to Pauline. Paul cut her down and tried to force life back into her. The police arrived with the paramedics. They call the coroner. Michael and Caroline tell the detectives their father was going to leave their mother for Laura. Paul hoped to persuade Michael and Caroline to accept Laura. The children were being prepared for a new arrangement in family life. He told them it would be *as if* they had two mothers. That's how Michael explains it to the police. I interrupted the plan by rejoining Laura in Madison, Pauline derailed it by killing herself.

At 7:00 that evening two detectives from the Madison Police Department come to our apartment. They flash their shields and want to interview Laura. She is in bed, trembling. My instinct is to protect her.

"She can't talk right now. My wife's under a doctor's care." I stand in the doorway.

Inspector Hawley is the lead detective. He again asks to speak with Laura. "This is police business. Do not interfere."

I move aside and invite them into the living room.

The phone in the hallway rings.

"Who is it?" Laura cries from the bedroom.

"It's Paul. He's calling from University Hospital and wants to talk with you. He's under observation."

Laura comes out into the hall in a pink flannel nightgown. Her eyes are ringed by dark shadows. Her wet hair lies matted against her skull. Paul does most of the talking and Laura keeps asking questions. "But where are the children? . . . How long will they keep you? . . . And you're back smoking? Please try to stop. . . . No, Paul, I can't do that now. . . . Please don't ask me to do that."

The detectives observe Laura, who barely notices them. When she hangs up, Laura turns to me. "God! He wants me to move into their house. Doesn't he realize others have feelings?"

31

Hawley steps forward and gives Laura his card. It is the scene from *Dragnet*. "Mrs. Ryan," he says, "Detective Pierce and I talked with the children Michael and Caroline Mason this afternoon. I have some questions to ask you about the deceased and want you to call me in the morning."

The detectives leave. Laura puts the card in her purse and goes back into the bedroom.

I call my sisters in Boston. Then I phone my friend Bob in Philadelphia. Bob knows the Masons. He's stunned by the news.

"Everything happens on Mondays," I tell him. "Pauline kills herself on a Monday. Laura's father dies on Monday. I spend the week trying to recover from Monday and meanwhile my work is not getting done. I hate Monday.

"Bob, I'm stuck in this craziness. Someone is dropping bricks on my head and I can't lift my arms to protect myself." Bob says he'll call back tomorrow, tells me to hang in there.

"Whom are you talking to?" Laura calls out from the bedroom.

"My sisters and Bob."

"They don't need to know all this."

I go to the bedroom door. Laura is sitting on the bed smoking in the dark.

"Why not? The rest of the world seems to. God, Laura, this is probably the worst day of my life. I need my friends."

The cigarette's glow brightens as she inhales. "Don't rag on me to your friends."

"You should find a lawyer before talking to the police."

"Just leave me alone. I don't want a lawyer."

She stubs the cigarette out and pulls the bedcovers up over her. I go back into the living room.

Friday, cont'd.

I will finish whatever remains between us. I call her back. I can't picture Laura, who's now fifty-three. I ask if she is healthy. "Healthy enough," she replies. I am looking for personal information, cues to help embody this voice that presumes to know me so well. Has her hair turned completely gray? I heard that some years ago. Does she experience orgasm? Is she smoking? How much weight has she put on? Does she like men or the vibrator more? But I'll learn nothing by asking directly. L: "I remember it all,

*David Ryan, I remember it all." This is her refrain.
D: "So do I but I put the horror of Madison and most of
those events behind. There's not much of a connection,
you know, between this life in California and when you
knew me some twenty-plus years ago." L: "I don't
consider myself married to you anymore." Where is she
coming from? The fact we were married in a Catholic
ceremony whose rules make it clear. For better or worse,
no matter which comes first. Married unto death.
No divorce. D: "When did you ever?"*

*Laura laughs. D: "So why did you apply for the annulment?" L: "To satisfy my mother," she says, "and why
did you object? You never wanted children. That alone is
grounds for an annulment in the Church." D: "I wouldn't
sign those forms for the marriage tribunal in Boston.
I read your petition for an annulment. The files lay open
on the priest's desk. He was kind enough to leave me
alone in the room with them. I grabbed the folder and
read through it. Your logic was strong, always coming
back to the point that I didn't want children and how that
is grounds for annulment. Nice reasoning there, organizing it into syllogisms to demonstrate that since ours was
not a valid marriage according to church teachings, your
now being married to Paul was irrelevant. You — citing
Canon Law. Really, Laura. Give me a fucking break. By
denying that any marriage between us ever existed, you
were free to do whatever you wanted to, like fucking Paul
and marrying him." L: "It wasn't remarriage for me.
Paul could have been the head waiter at Denny's.*

Paul wanted my ass." D: "And as usual, he got what he wanted. . ." L: "I would have gone with the grocer boy if he asked." D: "Yeah, you'd fuck him, too."

I need to talk about other things. D: "I met Hanna [Laura's sister] in Rockport a couple of summers after we separated. She was with her new husband, the doctor, and their children. They were touring the gift shops on Bearskin Neck." L: "She never mentioned it." D: "Really? . . Are they still together?" L: "No and my niece is about to get her MBA from Dartmouth." D: "Christ, it is that long ago. And Marlene?" L: "Eighty-one and full of life. She's living near my sister in Rhode Island." *She asks after my sisters and did not know Peggy died some years ago. No regrets at that news, just surprise.*

The Monona County coroner won't release the body. It has recently acquired bruises and an inquest into possible foul play is called for. The police advise Laura to find a lawyer. At the inquest, Detective Hawley reads Paul's statement into the record. Then Paul gives sworn testimony about trying to revive Pauline. He describes pounding on her chest and blowing air into her lungs. The Assistant DA corrects him. "Professor Mason, we are looking into bruises the deceased received while still alive. The Medical Examiner can tell the difference with the autopsy." He asks Paul about family violence. "Did he strike or punch her? Did she fall or bump into things?

Who was punishing this woman? . . . The deceased's body," he summarizes before the coroner's jury, "looked like an abused child's."

"The children know her of course, and they like her. I was trying to coax them into accepting the possibility of my marrying Laura." Paul denies what happened. "It has to be an accident." He explains why Pauline didn't want to kill herself. "She waited until she knew someone else would be up and find her. The kitchen stool must have slipped from underneath her." He insists Pauline wanted to be rescued. "She did this once before in Ithaca. I came home one afternoon and found her with her head in the oven. Pauline was groggy. She knew I was on the way home. I helped her outside and we walked around and around the block until her head cleared. . . . It has to be accidental. She didn't want to kill herself. She never said anything about suicide."

The DA asks how Pauline reacted to the likely separation.

"Yes, Pauline and I were discussing separation. She cried at first then seemed to accept the situation. Pauline was very concerned how the children would react. She didn't want them to be hurt. She was ready to divide the children's things so they'd feel at home, if Laura and I moved elsewhere. She was a good mother and wouldn't leave the children like this. Pauline did this to maneuver me into staying with her and her plan backfired."

There are hours of testimony. Laura and the Masons' neighbors are subpoenaed. Amos's wife Sarah collapses while testifying. The Medical Examiner reports that the deceased expired from asphyxiation caused by a cord tightened around her neck cutting off the oxygen and blood supply to her brain. "She was about four hours dead when I first examined the body. I estimate the time of death at or about 4:30 AM. Even if Professor Mason had managed to resuscitate her, the deceased's brain was already damaged from a deficit of oxygen and her mind most likely destroyed."

The inquiry is inconclusive. There is insufficient evidence to indict. Pauline's body is eventually released and shipped back to Pennsylvania for burial with her family in the Ukrainian cemetery outside of Scranton. A week later Sarah experiences a spontaneous miscarriage.

Laura and I talk about her feelings for Paul and whether we should stay married. She "wants to help Michael and Caroline." She never sees removing herself from their lives as an option. I look to survive the next three months until the semester ends, then escape to California. Perhaps we can resuscitate our marriage out there.

Laura agrees to come West. Then one day she says, "I have to see Paul again. I can't leave here without doing that. Just one final meeting, David. Please try to understand." Laura calls Paul on Sunday afternoon. They meet the next day for lunch.

It is Spring Break. Laura leaves the apartment wearing jeans and a navy turtle neck sweater and returns in about three hours. I am watching *American Bandstand*. Laura stands in front of the TV and switches it off.

"What did you have for lunch?"

"You want me. He wants me. I can't go on like this anymore. I want a divorce, David."

"What?"

"Need I repeat? I want a divorce."

Her words register like a punch to the temple. My brain is thudded.

"Those kids hate you."

"I'll live with that."

"You're fucking nuts to go with him."

"So I'm nuts."

I go for her throat. She gags and her face turns red then blue. My grip releases. The rib lines from the sweater leave marks on her neck. Laura grabs her purse and car keys and flees from the apartment. I uncover the IBM Selectric and begin arranging my research notes. When Laura returns about ten that night, I am typing. I type the next four months. Pauline perished in the middle of a messy situation. She is stuck in her mess. She will always be at the end of her rope. Writing a dissertation is a relief.

Friday, cont'd.

A wary ease surfaces between us. My years here in California brought new friendships and relationships, career change, a writing voice, etc. Most of my adult life has transpired in California. I lived with a woman I met in LA. We moved to San Francisco and were together for more than fourteen years. My life is different. I grew up.

I tell Laura about Susan and why I left. D: "I couldn't live with her drinking any longer." Laura knows nothing of this. Her relationship with me effectively ended the day she asked for a divorce. As far as I can tell, Laura never asked about me, never tracked my whereabouts the way I did hers. D: "I've been re-examining my experience with alcoholics in the past as well as the present. [Laura and I are children of alcoholics.] Being with Susan was the best relationship in my life. It was that good for years. We had many good times together. Yet it's no accident we got together." L: "Why wasn't it that way with me, David?" D: "Unlike you, Susan trusted me. The drinking continued so that changed everything." L: "You didn't try very hard to make our marriage work." D: "That was a long time ago, Laura. I did the best I knew. I've changed since then."

L: "Paul didn't cause the divorce." D: "Your involvement with Paul certainly didn't help." L: "Paul didn't cause our divorce, David." D: "Neither did I."

I just managed to survive childhood and first marriage. I want Laura's blaming to stop and won't listen to any more of it. D: "I was abused as a child and acted on what I believe was the thing to do. If I hurt you, Laura, sI am making amends right now."

There are no warm feelings left. The emotional contract is void and the middle of our bed has turned into a demilitarized zone. We sleep on the far edges. If her arm or leg brushes against me during sleep, I push or kick it away. "Stay on your side please." One has to be alert. My feelings for Laura are contradictory: wanting her as she was yet experiencing her in the present as spoiled meat. Contradictions may be unthinkable, but in the pain of a living being, contradiction has an actual existence. So says Hegel.

There is so much to say to Laura but I feel angry and betrayed. I want to talk about the horror of Pauline's death and ask Laura why she wants to be part of that family. It is now April. Laura goes to bed after coming home from her classes. I cook dinner and eat by myself. Laura gets up for a snack after I go to bed. She stays up for hours. The apartment reeks from cigarette smoke. The winter snow is nearly gone. Gray patches of the stuff remain in the back yard. The checkout girl at the Piggly Wiggly tells me the trees will remain bare another three or four weeks. After two weeks of silence, Laura says she is moving out. She won't give me her address and there will be no telephone listing.

"What if your mother calls?"

"I'll phone her from the office tomorrow and let her know how to reach me."

"What about the furniture and stuff?"

"Keep what you want. Put the rest into storage and send me the key."

Messages left with the departmental secretary are never answered. To reach Laura, I place notes on the car windshield in the faculty parking lot.

I'm moving from the apartment on Friday and can't take Henry where I'm going. I brought him to the county pound today. You have four days to claim him or they will gas him. The furniture is going to Bekin's Storage. Here's the receipt from the pound.

Friday, cont'd.

A couple of years ago I sent Laura a manuscript of poems. This is the one I most wanted her to see.

For Laura

80 poems
none about you
a painful chapter to reopen
none for the time
we were young married
beginning a life
away from our parents
tired hostility
we let them in
it's hard to write or
survive without shame
I remember your finale
I see us at 65 and bitter
rummaging through the past
there are hearty letters from a friend
wisecracks from another
Fort Dix is a seminary
lives setting out
in a few years we change
partners
then direction

One noontime I spot Paul in the Student Union. We don't speak but clearly he saw me. He is lunching with colleagues. Marcus the Department Chair is part of the group. The evening brings a phone call from Marcus. He wants to know how long I am going to be in Madison, and if there is anything he can do for me.

"When do classes start in California, David?"

"Late September."

"I'm glad you didn't say anything to Paul today. Seeing you upset him greatly."

"So what?"

"Harrington [the university Provost] fried our asses this morning. I'm to give him a monthly performance report on Paul. I was told to inform the tenured staff. That's what was going on at lunch today."

"Somebody should be monitoring him."

"Harrington wanted to know if Laura is leaving Madison. I told him I didn't know. She hasn't said much to me since resigning from the department."

"I haven't heard from her either, just her lawyer."

"I thought you'd have left Madison by now."

"What am I supposed to do, Marcus? Just pack up and

retreat. I never asked for any of this. I'm supposed to be writing the dissertation and there's other business to clear up here, too. What's more, I don't give a fuck about your burdens."

"No need to take out your anger on me, David. Pauline was a friend of ours, too. Paul saw you approaching us. He said, 'If Ryan talks to me, I'll strangle him.' I calmed Paul down and told him I'd talk with you. . . . I've got this headache that won't go away. Christ, Dave, I wish I never invited either of them here. I just don't know what's going to happen next with this situation."

"A little too late for regrets, Marcus. I still don't give a fuck."

Paul's words register as a threat, so I call Detective Hawley in the morning and report what Marcus said. I want the inquest reopened. I want that prick in jail.

"He threatened me."

"Remember Professor Mason was cleared of all wrongdoing. Pauline Mason hanged herself. She wasn't strangled."

"But he threatened me. His boss told me that."

"I'll talk with his boss."

Hawley also recommends I consider leaving early for California. "Get far away and keep away from that miserable son of a bitch." Hawley isn't looking for more business.

The following letter appears in the Madison *Capital Times*.

Dear Abby,
I've been with the same man for sixteen years. When we married, I was twenty-two and my husband twenty-five. I was a virgin but he wasn't. My husband spent three years in the Navy. He is now a teacher. On our vacation to France last summer he confessed that in the last five years he slept with four of his students. Now, every time we make love, I wonder who he's thinking about - and who he's comparing me with. It bothers me when we're out with friends and they start gossiping about which teachers are fooling around with the students. I wonder if they know about my husband's trysts. Are they laughing at me? How do I deal with this, Abby? I have forgiven my husband, but I am haunted by his infidelities. I feel that my life and the pain over my husband's infidelities are nothing.

Distressed

Abby recommends to Distressed that she seek counsel from her clergyman right away and get into therapy.

I see Paul another noontime as he was leaving the Union. There is no direct contact (too many people around) and once again in a line for a movie with Michael and Caroline. Same blue velour shirt, chinos, etc. Paul avoids eye contact, making it obvious he doesn't want to talk. He turns away as I begin walking towards him. If the children hadn't been with Paul, I would have thrown a punch at him.

His cool demeanor irritates me. I want to get my hands on him. He acts as if recent events have no affect. Never expressed regrets or took any responsibility that I am aware of. I look for him to acknowledge in some way the pain he caused. Paul told Amos he didn't believe in ghosts. That's all he had to say. Pauline is history.

Marcus's wife, Selda, is the hostess for the reception at the Masons' house after the memorial. Amos and Sarah are there; her stomach bulges with life. The children are outside on the patio. Caroline holds on to a brown rag doll. Michael straddles a bench and plays solitaire.

"I'm worried about her, Paul," Laura says.

"My children are happy if I'm happy."

I find his concern questionable. The rest of us are satellites. That's what I conclude.

Perhaps this is to be expected. Paul's book, The *Analysis of Value* (University of the Prairies Press, 1965), demonstrates how "good answers to an interest."

He is a good soldier.

Treachery is good.

Laura is good.

Paul is good.

Paul has the argumentative skills to prove himself right — with interest.

Nearing

she wants my attention
wants me to face her
diverts me from pursuing more
she asks where is your home
where is your place to rest
who will take care of you when I come again
who cares if you leave and don't return
this visit now much more
than casual contact with a pretty woman

experience tells me to respect power
she demands her place
David, she says, look me in the eye
say if you can it doesn't matter
say you don't care
say you don't fear me

Laura and I meet as undergrads at Boston College. Both of us high achievers. I first notice her when she played Goody Proctor in "The Crucible." She is clearly the most talented performer. Laura's a campus star with her pick of men. Even then her black hair has a few gray strands. Olive complexion and dark eyes. Roman nose. Slender. Well breasted. I fanaticize. Laura seems carefree, immune to the weather. I have an image of her running through an April snow shower in a light sweater. Her favorite Spring outfit is a peasant dress with a tight-fitting green velvet dirndl that shows off her breasts. Laura audits Victorian literature. Many days she slides into the next seat to share my textbook. I get excited. Her mood difficult to predict. She speaks if we meet on campus or doesn't.

Marriage soon after graduation is the fashion. Laura plans to join her fiancé, a graduate student at Stanford. Then he breaks their engagement with a long distance call. My passion is Nancy. Her attorney father is an unlucky gambler. She goes to the nearby Catholic women's college where her role models are celibate nuns.

Nancy has a music scholarship but hesitates to try for a career as a singer. "It's too up and down," she tells me. "I know what it's like to live in apparent affluence and have the phone shut off because the bill is unpaid. I watch my stepmother deal with no money. That's not for me."

Nancy turns me on. She's a little chunky with dark hair and pale Irish skin. We date for about eighteen months. Everything possible except the thing that intimacy is to bring about. We pet in the library stacks. We neck on park benches in Boston Common. My balls just about to burst. Her cunt soft, turning gelatinous, yet we always stop just short.

Some barriers are impenetrable. Nancy believes that just fondling her breasts will make her pregnant. I try explaining otherwise because I want into Nancy. Guilt routinely overwhelms Nancy. She would go to confession to quiet the prick of conscience. The next time we French kiss or touch each other's genitals, a fresh attack of remorse sweeps over her. She is topping me.

Nancy agonizes until her period begins. We break up soon after graduation. She goes looking for a husband with better economic prospects and dates men from Harvard and MIT. I take a job at the National Security Agency in Washington. I'm not supposed to mention that.

The second spring after graduation. The government job is over. I move back in with my sisters, moping around the house not really knowing what I should do next. I miss the excitement of being with Nancy. My sister Peggy suggests, "Why not call that girl who came to Rockport last summer with Jim Murphy?" *That girl* is Laura.

Laura stayed at Boston College for a Master's in Philosophy and I begin visiting the campus. I stake out the cafeteria. We meet on the stairs.

"What a surprise, Laura. I've been thinking about you."

"I heard you were in Washington."

"I left."

"What is being a spy like?"

"It's political. The phones are bugged. My supervisor lectured me and even wrote me up after a girl spent a weekend in my apartment. . . . No privacy and the agency is doing a lot of things I don't like. . . . You never knew whom you were talking to. I can't say much about it."

"You mean if you tell me you might have to kill me?" She laughs.

"Absolutely."

"And your girlfriend from Regis?"

"It was over when I left for Washington. For the moment I'm subbing in the Boston schools. No call for work this morning, so I walked over here."

"Too bad. You two looked so chummy."

I laugh at her use of *chummy*. She says she watched Nancy and me smooching in the library courtyard.

"I was envious," she says.

This is a good moment between us.

"What about that guy at Stanford?"

"We broke up."

Laura tells me about the phone call and her futile trip to California to rescue the engagement. "He just didn't want marriage to me anymore." She laughs. "Oh well, on to the next."

We begin dating. Laura lives in her parents' home near Cambridge. Many Sunday afternoons we walk through the grounds of Mt. Auburn Cemetery. Memorials to famous Bostonians materialize at each turn of the road. William and Alice James. Longfellow. Mary Baker Eddy. Amy Lowell. We walk along mansion row on Brattle Street. Tea and desserts in the Blacksmith Shop. With the right breaks, we could have a gracious life.

We discuss graduate schools. Laura wants a Ph. D. I want to study literature and write. We search for a suitable place. Once both of us get accepted at Penn, we become engaged and marry — all within a few months. Marriage represents our decision to live and work together. Laura is, I believe, my last and only chance for love.

Friday, cont'd.

Laura says she is two months back from a sabbatical year in England. She traveled alone and stayed in a dormitory. L: "Remember how I wanted to study at Oxford. I talked about it the summer we were dating." She has my business card, which I enclosed in a manuscript I mailed her about two years ago. She got my new phone number from information. She comments on the poems. "Odd," she says, "odd how little there is of you in there. So much mirroring of other people." She says I never loved her. "I remember it all, David," she says every so often to reinforce a point, "I remember it all."

I tell Laura how I used to imagine unexpectedly meeting her. Possibly in the Crossroads of the World Bar at O'Hare Airport. We would run into each other in a layover between connecting flights. L: "I did see you once, you know. You have a mustache." D: "Had. That was my disguise in the sixties and seventies. The revolution is long dead." L: "You looked the same pugnacious self." D: "My side lost so I shaved it off - years ago. I look younger."

Two summers after the divorce, I went back East and sublet an apartment near Harvard Square. D: "I thought I once saw you at a table in that outdoor cafe in front of the Brattle Theatre." I remember that jump I felt in my chest when I spotted anyone who looked like her. D: "I kept walking for another block, not quite believing it was you, and when I got to the corner of Church Street and turned back whoever that was had left. I checked inside the cafe, too." L: *"Yes, that was me."* D: *"Christ, Laura, I was sort of going crazy then and convinced myself that I had projected your image onto someone else. I can hardly believe it."* L: *"I didn't want to meet you."* D: *"We used to spend time together in Harvard Square. I was still distraught about what happened. . . . I thought the past was overwhelming the present. Now you tell me."* L: *"I felt that if I talked to you, David, you might try to kill me again."* D: *"You may be right. But killing you was never worth it."*

In my head I count up the bills from therapists in LA and San Francisco. That jump in my chest comes back along with the memory of the scene in Harvard Square. I want Laura to reveal more of herself. I still need an image. I tell Laura how Susan and I lived together in San Francisco for almost fourteen years. D: *"Susan was very jealous of you. I probably talked about you too much, especially when we were first together. . . . I used to track your whereabouts, you know, the schools you taught at, looked for your name in the journals. Every so often I'd go to the Philosophy Library at Berkeley and scan them for mentions of you or Paul. Fortunately I got over that. You still aren't in* Books in Print. *Never publish a book and still get tenure. How did you arrange that?"* L: *"I didn't sleep with anyone, if that's what you're asking."* D: *"Just curious, Laura. . . . You know I was visiting friends in South Carolina a few years ago after a business trip to*

Atlanta. Susan thought I went East to see you. She was probably drinking." L: "When we were at Chapel Hill?" D: "Yeah. I couldn't disabuse her of the notion. Susan called me at the Matalene's house. 'Is Laura there?', she kept asking. I tried explaining I was in <u>South</u> not North Carolina."

I tell these facts to let her know how long it took me to get over her suddenly exiting the marriage and taking up with Paul. We talk for nearly an hour. The seriousness gradually lightens. The more Laura and I talk the less guarded I feel and before the end of our conversation I even thank her for calling. That was a little much, but talking with her did clear up some old business.

In bed on the verge of sleep I have a strange bodily experience. A large bright spot covers my chest, extending from the top of the breast bone to a point below the navel. The spot looks like a scar that is healing. I fall asleep giggling.

Saturday, October 1   8:00 PM

Trivial events sometimes trigger rich, complex memories. As I walk over the hill to the Tassajara Cafe in the Haight this morning, I recall our delight when Susan and I first discover this San Francisco neighborhood. One memory evokes other memories of how Susan redefined reality. She continued to insist that mayonnaise contains protein, even after I read her the label on the jar. S: "It does and it *doesn't, David." When the Muni was stringing new overhead wires in our neighborhood for the electric buses, Susan didn't like it. D: "But it's less polluting and no noise. There's no diesel exhaust." S: "It's visual pollution. And it's killing me."*

When we ate out, I ask for a nonsmoking table. If there wasn't one available, we'd wait at the bar. As her drinking increased, eating out became problematic. She'd have two or three drinks before dinner and then order a carafe of wine with the meal. I was drinking more than I wanted so I began cutting back. Meaningful conversation became scarcer. "It's not the food, David," she'd say, "but the experience of eating out." I waved away the smoke from her cigarette. I began ordering wine by the glass. Susan guessed right it was a strategy to get her to drink less.

Reveille

I sit in the cold morning sun
the fire won't catch and who will help
I call them. Susan is dead.
She is also sleeping
in the bedroom without sound.
Give me a hand with the body.

Saturday, cont'd.

I remain critical of Susan, loathe her personal habits, yet miss her company. She is a warm and gifted woman, an interior architect. We met in a therapy group in LA. I loved sleeping over in her apartment. Her way with colors and textures enticed me. Large stuffed couches and a soft bed with a down comforter. I'd cuddle next to Susan, reassured after making love. I needed a home. My friends became her friends, then our friends.

The window sills in her kitchen held an array of green and clear onion-shaped bottles from the Almaden winery. She was sprouting gardenias and philodendron in them.

We began living together, then moved to San Francisco where I found a job. We furnished an apartment in the Marina. I had a home again. Susan loved Christmas and insisted on a tree. My resistance to the holidays — they are still difficult — melted. Almost every Christmas we held open house for our Cafe Flore friends.

It is warm and humid. We sleep in the nude and lie on our left sides. The windows are open and the shades up. I reach over her for the primrose oil on the night table. Squeeze some into my hands to coat my fingers. The oil is body temperature. My right hand goes into her crotch and I begin to softly roll the labia between my fingers then dart my greased index finger into her anus with effect. She stirs, still sleepy, and turns over.

We kiss and she places her right hand against my face. Her thumb traces the outline of my lips. My finger moves in and out of her anus. The edge of her nail runs against the tip of my tongue. I suck on her thumb and massage more oil into her. She turns moist. She reaches for the lotion and massages my testicles. I stay firm and hard. She guides my cock into her, squeezing the stem, almost cutting off feeling, to slow my coming. I cup her left breast and roll the nipple. Her finger circles my anus then slides in and out. Come inside me, please come. Our hips grind against each other's. She releases her grip. The cum surges up my penis and out like water spraying out of a lawn sprinkler.

Those wine bottles along the sunny kitchen windows were clues that didn't register. I never asked why there were so many or thought much about who emptied them. The sprouting plants and flowers kept my attention.

Monday, October 3   *9:00 PM*

Sunday night I was back in bed with another bout of flu. Someone pokes a hole high up on the wall near the ceiling and peers through the hole into the room. He observes me sleeping. I stir awake to see him pull his head back when I look up. I reach for the phone to notify the landlord. Someone has broken in, I tell him. The dream startles me.

I am seldom ill. One more surge of partially digested material erupts. I make it to the bathroom in time. When I do get sick, though, the figure of my mother, caring yet cautionary, returns. She nursed me through measles, chicken pox, and appendicitis. Once again I hear her saying, "Hold on, don't lose control of yourself, don't make a mess." Slept almost twelve hours. My stomach aches today like the ache felt after exercising seldom used muscles.

In mid-afternoon I go out for air and refreshment. Ride the Muni over to my old neighborhood near the Bay and get a haircut. Feeling very spruced up. Then I see Susan on the other side of Union Street. A failed dream. I cross over to her, after she had seen me and turned away. The changes are disturbing. She moves stiffly and her complexion has a gray pallor. I keep looking at her even when there is little to say. She has not worked for a year, she says, and has stopped looking. Her blotched face sprouts a goatee. Who would hire her? D: "You don't look healthy." S: "I'm not wearing foundation."

If Susan asked me for anything today, a loan for instance, and I refused her, I might feel guilty. I keep looking at her because I want the image to sink in. She notices. S: "It's my dirty hair. I didn't wash it this morning." Her mouth is drawn. She has dentures. The lipstick unevenly applied. I remember a wide smile and rich throaty laugh. I visualize Susan with the expression and features she bore when we lived together, not with those of the person she has become. She was so open to the world. I stare at her. The Susan I knew is no longer. More than the changes that age brings. The changes that disease brings.

Life with Susan

3 stories up we lie in bed
your smells hit me
I sleep next to a snoring and sweaty corpse
more sodden voices from the street
2 AM and the drunks roll uphill
from the Union Street bars
Todd is coaxing Muffie into his car
leave yours here and pick it up in the morning
we ignore each other
for 30 minutes the sprinklers chatter
evicting a pair of fat coons
from the ivy and iceplant
the pain of our neighbors
we're renters and not of their class
the woman I loved is not here

I delay leaving Madison, still hoping Laura might wake from this nightmare and join me in California. I wait for her to flee Paul and the children. To keep sane I create routines such as translating one hundred lines of Latin each morning. I need the order of declensions. Some days the choice is *Ars Poetica*, some days the satires of Jerome. Women are a favorite scourge. By 9:30 AM the mental exercises are done.

I make my own way in Madison, inhabiting a world apart from the Philosophy Department. I move to a rooming house where I spend days writing the dissertation. Most nights I go to the 602 Club, the bar with the bad reputation, where I ran into an acquaintance from Boston. I like having a joint to go to.

Jane is a graduate student in sociology. She was a Red Diaper baby. Jane invites me to share meals at her eating co-op, where the comrades berate Trotskyites and Maoists much the same way my mother and her relatives served up their memories of British atrocities in Ireland with roast beef and mashed potatoes. Telling these stories over Sunday dinner was routine when I was growing up. Marxist differentiation is beyond me, however. Catholicism defined a sufficiently wide array of moral categories and human transgressions. I am unwilling to take on one more abstraction. *Je suis marxiste tendance groucho.* They are not amused. Jane recruits me to help organize the anti-war movement on campus. There are demonstrations and "Uncle Ho" rallies. I have energy and anger to channel. I join a guerrilla theater group. We write and produce agitprop. My Boston accent plays well in the Midwest, so I get to be JFK or one of the Ivy-League toadies populating the State Department.

The collective is planning a memorial to those being killed in Vietnam. There are nights of slicing white fiberboard, stapling the pieces into crosses, and printing a name on each. We copy the names from the *Capital Times*, which publishes every month the cumulative list of those killed in the war. The body count was reaching 9,000. We meet in Jane's apartment before dawn one Monday morning to transport the crosses to the campus. I slip three more into the batch with Paul's, Pauline's, and Laura's names. Each is better off dead. A different cadre surveyed the site (they told the university police they were doing it for a landscaping class) and laid out a grid with strings on the sloping lawn leading up to Bascom Hall. We will plant the crosses there. By the time the students are on the way to their eight o'clock classes, the slope looks like a military cemetery.

It is difficult to link Paul and Laura to the enemies of the movement. He is politically correct. If he did support the war, however, that would be one more reason to despise him. His name and university affiliation routinely appear with other academics' in the anti-war advertisements in the *New York Times*. In May I join the sit-in at the Administration building. A couple of thousand students ring the building and fill the hallways. Twenty of us seize the Provost's office. Plaques from county farm associations and awards from fraternal organizations such as the Rotary and Kiwanis cover a wall in Harrington's office. I try on Harrington's hacking jacket, lean back in his Eames chair, and pass out the Cuban cigars from the humidor on the desk.

My eyes scan the office ceiling as I replay from memory Marcus's account of the meeting with Harrington. It happened right here. I appoint myself the new Provost.

"What are you thinking about, David?" Jane asks me.

I take a long drag on the cigar and flick the ash on the carpet.

"What's going on?"

"You know I'd like to borrow some of Harrington's power. There are people around here who could use more pain in their lives. Whenever he likes to, Harrington makes others dance to his tune."

Jane looks puzzled.

"You're getting weirder, David."

I take another drag on the cigar, put my feet back up on the desk and exhale. Jane only knew I was getting divorced, nothing about the personalities involved. She called my behavior unstable in her report to the collective.

The View From Elaine's Porch

From this distance
on the occasionally shared morning
there's a fat green tub filled with gas
stalagmites of glass and steel downtown
a miniature container ship floating
the Bay Bridge sags over a pond
you are in your kitchen cleaning
the PG&E chimney on the horizon
appears inflamed
turns redder at the top
Mt. Diablo slumbers
one day it will start oozing
to reclaim privacy you say
I am a morning person
I'm eager for the view
we disagree when I should leave
so I breathe in your spirit
remembering how I cup
your breasts in my hands
We have no luck with restaurants
I cook and can do better
send it back, says my friend the chef
don't accept poorly done food
always send it back
I like full meals
usually clean my plate
you eat less and are ready
to have your day

Sunday, October 9   *9:15 AM*

Elaine and I continue dating. She remains detached. There are pleasant interludes. A night of intense dreams. We are touring the Northern California coast. Three people share the front seat of a VW bus. Our luggage is piled high in the back. I sit in the middle with the gear shift between my legs. Elaine is on my right. She keeps sliding down into the space between the edge of the seat and the door. She feels less than complete. Martha, a friend of Elaine's, a large, stern, uncommunicative woman with metal-frame glasses, drives. She grunts when she reaches for the gear shift and slams it into second. She's wearing a man's gray shirt, jeans, and will not relinquish the driving. I hesitate to touch or fondle Elaine in front of her. We are subject to Martha's dominance.

The scenery along the coast highway is periodically transformed. One moment the view resembles Rockport, Massachusetts, where my sisters live and where they first met Laura with Jim Murphy. Another turn on the coastal highway and the prospect resembles Monterey, California, where Elaine's parents retired. We arrive at a white Victorian hotel. Inside the lobby a Tiffany glass canopy encircles the ornate bar. Embedded in the canopy are legends of local interest such as "Mule State College" and "Big Bend River." A sign on the wall points out where we are. 'The-City-of-Texas-in-California-on-the-Big-Bend-River.' Under the sign there's an antique surveyor's map of the state of Texas with the course of a winding river traced across it. This site in California gets its name from its topological resemblance to Big Bend, Texas.

Peggy

>she is here so we talk
>of separation
>and what is left behind
>the spirit visits
>here when I look
>vanishing
>if I question
>presence
>the world feels less
>we agree death is awesome
>the body never again alive
>the days go on
>we meet and talk

Sunday, cont'd.

In a different dream segment, I am on the beach at Big Sur talking to someone seated inside a shuttered hot dog stand. His face remains hidden, like the priest's inside the confessional booth. "My friend Raphael is the father of Michelle's illegitimate child, and Susan is pregnant by him, too." The conversation shifts to Paul. "I should have killed him when I had the chance." My sister Peggy appears, looking spent and haggard as she walks slowly along the beach. I tell Peggy about Laura. "The bitch finally called. I had to tell her you died."

Lunar

I feel the draw of the moon. I must be out. These teeth he said running the tip of his tongue from one incisor across to the other these teeth are sensitized. I dress in black and must be out cruising.

I remember one winter night on Boston Common. The snow ice crackled as he walked his girlfriend to a park bench next to the Frog Pond. Old snow speckled with grime lined the cement crater. The icy sidewalks pick up the gray moonlight. Nowhere we can go to smooch and fondle. We had to be out shivering buried in overcoats. A hand in through the sweater and down into her pants. It was cold and hard to warm up Nancy.

The moon at Big Sur seen from the Casita at the edge of a cliff. The line of light on the corrugated water. Stand on the cabin deck look over and down. Waves smashing. Forces slower than one lifetime erode the person. Always here. The surf swirls through a natural bridge at the base of a cliff. The arch in the moonlight from the deck.

I see Laura once again before leaving for California. I am having Saturday morning coffee at Rasmussen's and staring out the window. There she is, crossing State Street hand-in-hand with Michael and Caroline. Laura wears the Irish knit sweater Peggy gave her. I run outside. She is uncomfortable. The children clutch Laura's hands and keep looking at her as we talk.

"How you doing, Laura?"

"I'm all right . . . and you."

I rehearsed my speech for her so many times and this is not the meeting I anticipated. It's difficult to say anything in front of the children. I also feel abandoned.

"I'm leaving for Philadelphia next week to turn in my first draft of the dissertation and take my orals. Then it's off to California." I have to ask. "Why don't you come?"

"I can't," she says, "I have three people to take care of. The children need me."

"Who's the third?"

"Paul. He's smoking again and I'm scared of what it's doing to his health."

I want to ask her when the affair with Paul first began and if she was fucking him while we were at Penn. The children's presence deters me. Laura says goodbye and they head for the parking garage. This is our last meeting.

The following Spring my sister Peggy visits me in California. She tells me that Laura and Paul are married.

Monday, October 10   *1:30 PM*

When I relate the dream to my friend Bob, he notes its key figures are the women in my life. At first I didn't identify Elaine as the girlfriend sitting next to me in the VW. Then I recall Elaine wore a green blouse Saturday night; in the dream she is wearing a green sweater. Elaine does not want to use "love" for our friendship and holds back. Bob says I know all the women represented in the dream. Susan is from Texas but we met in LA. The Big Bend may represent the almost 180-degree turn in my life since I left her. In the dream my sister Peggy talks from the side of her mouth. Her speech distorted by Bell's palsy. This is how she looked during the final weeks of her life.

Bob says the dream is a review of the anima, *my inner representation of the female. Bob asks, "In what ways do these women resemble your mother, David?"*

"They have painful lives. . . . My mother believed great pain was her lot. She was always saying her rosary; she was drawn to the Sorrowful Mysteries. Every Wednesday she'd trek across Boston to the Mission Church for the novena to Our Lady Of Perpetual Help. Fr. Manton

preached and said Benediction. The women adored him. She looked forward to dying, because it would bring relief. She was a living saint with leg ulcers for stigmata.

"*'Some day, David,' my mother would say in low moments, 'some day all this will be over.'*" Holy Mary, Mother of God, pray for us now and at the hour of our death. And, please God, let it be soon. Amen. *Amen.*

Right Living

shall I confess
shall I purge
forget the cold
worn man
untouching
fearful
and herself
mother pope
and church
storming
against sin
against pleasure
praying to
her special Jesus
pledging her son
to love Jesus
her care
still binds

>
> her prayers
> answered
> as he walked
> the first time
> the fiction
> of miracle
> an unceasing
> burden

Every so often a letter arrives or a call to friends who are still teaching. I bailed out of academia about twelve years ago. Bob remains a source of much news. According to him, Laura and Paul stayed together until Caroline finished high school. Then Laura divorced Paul. Laura moved to New York, married again and divorced again. She has tenure at a university on Long Island. Last year Bob wrote that Paul retired and moved to Tempe for his emphysema.

Saturday, October 15   *Noon*

Dear Laura,

Thanks for breaking the ice. Our talk is a significant event in my life. If we did it, say twenty years ago, I might have saved 1000's of $$$ in therapy.

David

On the reverse of the postcard is a picture of the Buddha in Golden Gate Park. His palm is raised in peaceful greeting and fresh flowers rest at the base. I write the same message on another card with an aerial view of Alcatraz. I stand in front of the mail box debating which to send.

An event at work prompts these memories of more than twenty years ago. I changed careers some time ago and work as a systems analyst with Xerox in Palo Alto. Each month Human Resources posts on the lunchroom bulletin board photos with brief bios of new employees in our division. Two young women I work with, René and Tami, stand next to the bulletin board rating the new employees over coffee and cigarettes.

"Oh this one's cute," says Tami, "take a look."

"His ears are too big."

"Check this hunk, René. Those eyes. Yum."

What makes women prefer some men over others? Their selections are as puzzling as the ones I've made. Paul wasn't known for integrity. Was his dick that hard, that big? On the way back to my workstation I scan the bulletin board. The strong features and deep-set eyes of one new hire look familiar. He has his father's eyes.

Michael Mason - Midwest Sales

```
Michael joins Xerox as the new Educa-
tion Sales Rep in the Chicago region.
He attended the University of North
Carolina.  Michael has over eight
years' experience in selling and mar
keting business equipment and office
automation systems. His last posi-
tion was with Itek Graphix. Welcome
to Xerox, Michael!
```

Monday, October 17

Edith left a message on the machine. She wants to know who wrote, "You ask me, why, though ill at ease,/Within this region I subsist,/ Whose spirits falter in the mist." She thought it was Tennyson. She's right. The poem's in the Norton Anthology. A photo dated August 1963 is stuck in the book. My sister Peggy, Laura, and I are standing in front of her parents' home. I'm between Peggy and Laura, my arm resting on Laura's shoulder. I look young and trim, my face thin and unlined. Laura is photogenic. She wears a thin-strapped summer dress. Her hair is cut short. No shadow of what lay in store for us. Not a trace of shame or the abysmal lack of self-confidence I was then experiencing. No hint of distrust in Laura's body language. No premonitions. Peggy looks robust and is quietly smiling, no sign of drunken bingeing. Our genuinely disarming closeness is obvious. Looking into the camera. Posing for the photographer.

Tuesday, October 18   *8:00 PM*

After revising the story, I send it to Laura. Wonder how she'll react. She has her own version of events. She'll remembers it all, too. I mail Bob a copy.

The girl of my dreams is no longer available
she shed that nineteen year-old's body
and took on a mature woman's
her breasts set somewhat lower
her buns sink behind the knees
and she's living with a sixty year-old man
I scribble notes and dial long distance
my calls don't get through
postcards return stamped "Whereabouts Unknown"

That girl, the one I married, was in my dream
just last night. We were in the Museum
admiring each other and Matisse's
The Woman in the Red Hat
I was about to fondle Odalisque's soft body

Wednesday, October 19 *2:30 PM*

Susan may have disappeared. From across the street I can see into her apartment and it is empty. One rainy night last week I went to the movies at the Metro on Union Street. Susan's apartment is right around the corner on Webster Street. The drapes billow out the open windows. No lights. Now, a week later, the windows are shut and the drapes gone. I see what looks like a box spring on its side. I nearly write "our" box spring. She is no longer living here and I have no way of knowing where to look. She may be dead, she may be hospitalized.

Susan kept a schedule, shuttling between her apartment and the nearby bars. I could count on spotting her almost any Saturday afternoon as I walked along Union Street.

I'd peer into the Deli Bar to find her perched on a stool, hunched over a glass of white wine. Such predictability was reassuring and I used it to validate my decision to leave her. I made a game of whether I would look for her or whether I would walk by and disregard her. I invented variations on the game. I practiced walking by the bar and not looking. I practiced looking. If I found her, I'd go the corner, turn around, walk by the bar again and this time not look. I practiced detaching.

Friday, October 28

A note from Bob.

Dear David,

Some first impressions. I'm about halfway through your piece. You are having difficulty distinguishing between two completely different kinds of writing . . . between a subjective work that is trying to reach an artistic form using real events as its basis, and a documentary that professes to present everything without error.

More later.

Bob

Friday, November 4

A letter from Laura arrives. My senses jump when I see her printed handwriting.

David:

Your note about saving money on therapy is smarmy. And why the second postcard? Did you forget mailing the first? Maybe you've been smoking too much California sensimillia. Your story about me (I'm presuming Laura is me) is irritating and untruthful. Paul did not break up

*our marriage. You did when you pulled away from me,
when you decided not to move to Madison with me that
September but returned to Philadelphia, presumably to
complete your dissertation and get a good job. That decision
alone killed my feeling for you. I no longer wanted to live
with you yet couldn't bring myself to say I want a divorce.
I knew you'd be hurt. Paul meant nothing to me. You had
turned away from me and he was available (as always).
Pauline did not kill herself nor was Paul likely to batter her.
Her death was not premeditated. Pauline was trying to
frighten Paul and me. Furthermore, I don't recall any of that
stuff about Amos and Sarah.*

*What did my parents have to do with our marriage? They
left us alone. Yes, Marlene can be bitchy but she is an old
woman now and doesn't need reminders of her past. Please
don't contact her. Why not write about your own parents
and their violent relationship? David, I was a virgin when I
married you and believed we would be together for life. That
was the vow I made. That was the promise that I thought
you made to me. I wanted to have children and a family
with you. You said you did too - at first. But once we were
married and away from Boston, you changed your mind.*

*You tried to stop me from going to church after we moved
to Philadelphia. You made light of my faith. Those were
my grounds for seeking the annulment. I no longer practice
Catholicism or pay attention to its rules. But I once did,
David, and you maliciously undermined me. Why are you
continuing to rake over the past? What's your point?*

I can't stop you from distributing your story or publishing it. At least get the facts straight. I'm thinking of calling a lawyer.

Laura
P.S. Please don't re-introduce yourself to Michael. Your connection to those children is remote. Let Michael keep that period of his life to himself.

I sent Laura the story to get her to re-examine the events. The only effect is that she will consult a lawyer. Let her sue. Fuck her.

Tuesday, November 8

Dream. My life suddenly brightens after meeting a woman. She is tall and slender with dark hair. We drive down to Big Sur and stay overnight at the Ventana Inn. (The feeling of light resplendence is more intense than any other event in the dream, even our sleeping together.) *Perhaps the dream is connected to meeting Ivy again last night. She has an uncommon effect on me; it is cumulative. Ivy is young and slender. She's bisexual. I didn't want our meeting to end. I didn't want to break away. As I was leaving Edith's house last night, I kept turning back to Ivy, saying goodbye again and again. I went over to her and hugged her before I left.*

Wednesday, November 9

A second letter arrives.

David:

You may believe you are writing about a divorce almost thirty years in the past but you seem to overlook the plain fact that you write mainly about yourself. No one could have written that scenario of Pauline's suicide but you (or me), and I cannot see why you feel it is necessary. I would like to know what purpose you think this tale is going to serve.

I want to thank you for making me face the very real and terrible possibility that, if we had continued to live together, I would be one more academic woman who sublimates motherhood by influencing other women's children. Michael and Caroline were the closest I came to having children.

Slander is no less slander for being a fact.

Laura